THE TRUE ADVENTURES OF
ECZEMA MAN

BY ISAAC GARONZIK

THE TRUE ADVENTURES OF ECZEMA MAN

TABLE OF CONTENTS

CHAPTER 1

THE DAY I BECAME ME

"You okay?" asked Coach Tim.

I didn't know how he could tell.

I looked at him with a smile. "Of course." I had my semi-final playoff baseball game that day, but my eczema had been hurting me so much lately. I was the best pitcher in our league, and I was pitching horribly in one of the biggest games of the season.

"Time!" shouted Coach Tim.

As my coach and infield surrounded the mound, I could see my teammates paralyzed with fear. Anthony (our first baseman and my best friend) yelled out to me, "Yo Jimbo Limbo, what's wrong?"

"It's my hands. My eczema's hurting me more than ever." My hands were chapped, and some parts were even bleeding where my skin cracked.

"Do you want to stop?" Coach asked me.

"No!" exclaimed Cameron, our second baseman and the fastest hot dog eater I knew. "Jimmy is the Babe Ruth of our league."

Coach shouted out words I had never heard him shout at me before. "You've walked three guys in a row. One more, and you are out of here Jimmy."

Everyone walked back to their positions. I thought to myself: *Last inning, two outs, and a season to keep alive. Giving up another walk would lose us the game.*

I was going up against the biggest jerk in school, Fred Winkelstein. He bullied everyone. He once tried to trip Anthony during lunch; he threw spitballs at my friends Emma and Virginia in math class; and he always called people bad names. Earlier in the season, I hit him with a pitch just so he would leave my friends and me alone. My parents were both in the stands cheering me on. I looked at my dad for comfort, but all he did was mouth the words "Stay Calm." I looked at home plate, went through my wind up, and threw the ball.

"Strike One," called the umpire.

I got the ball back and thought about what dad had mouthed to me. I took a deep breath and went back into my wind up. I threw the ball with all the power I could muster. I heard the umpire again. "Strike Two."

At that point, my eczema was making me feel like one hundred wasps were stinging my hands all at once. I was sure I would have to go to the hospital directly after the game. My eczema was killing me. My pitching hand was burning, and my other hand was making my fingers itch inside of my glove. I realized I only needed one more strike. I threw down the pitch in a slow pace so my hand wouldn't hurt. Let's just say, IT FAILED! It bounced before the plate. Okay. 1-2 count.

The next time, I put more power into my pitch than I ever thought I could. I threw the ball with every ounce of might I had and looked away, hoping to hear Strike Three. But I heard nothing. Not a sound.

No cheering.

No clapping.

Nothing.

I also felt nothing.

No burning.

No itching.

Nothing.

My hands actually didn't itch; they didn't burn. It was instant relief.

There was silence. And then more silence.

I looked down at my pitching hand, my right hand. It made no sense. My eczema was gone. It was cured totally out of the blue. I looked up to see why nobody had said anything. Then I heard lots of things coming from the stands. Really really loud voices were shouting.

"Run . . . run!"

"Call 911!"

"Get the news station."

"Get the police."

"Call an ambulance!"

My friend Randy, the catcher, was completely covered in what looked like cobwebs. All I could see through his catcher's mask were his eyes staring at me. It was at that moment that I noticed it. It wasn't a cobweb, but it sure looked like one. It was white, and it was wrapped all over Randy's head and arms. It looked like white snakes were slithering up and down his legs. Then it hit me. I checked my hands once more, saw they were clear, and looked up. Randy was covered with my eczema!

I had put so much power into my pitch that my eczema literally shot out of me. The webs all over Randy were my peeled skin. I was so amazed that I ran to my team's bench, grabbed a baseball, and chucked it as far and hard as I could toward a tree. The ball traveled at the fastest speed I had ever seen, and it was covered with eczema. It hit the tree's brown trunk, and the tree trunk turned completely white. Everyone looked at me. The stadium was silent.

I heard some chatter. Then someone screamed louder than I had ever heard, "Help! He's a monster."

My dad and mom ran to the bench to check on me. All I could do was look at my hands. My glove laid on the floor as I examined how smooth and soft my hands felt for the first time all season. I told my parents I was happy, but deep down I was sad. People were talking about me, not in a good way. Not the way they usually talked about my fast pitches or how quickly I stole bases. They were talking about how much I scared them. I could see it in their faces.

Suddenly, I heard sirens. A police van approached the field, followed by an ambulance, followed by a news truck.

CHAPTER 2

OCTAGON ISN'T JUST A SHAPE

A news reporter exited the truck. She approached me, fixed her hair, and started asking questions. The reporter made this seem like a planned interview. She had a list of questions and used the field as the backdrop for the scene.

"Hello friends, I am Katelyn Fox here with Jimmy Mancini. Jimmy, you just threw an eczema ball. How did you do it?"

I answered with lots of fear in my voice, "It was very peculiar. I have no idea. I can't explain it."

She responded, "Jimmy, normal people can't do that. Why can you? You know what that means? Jimmy, you're a superhuman. With that comes big responsibilities. Do you understand the importance of your actions?"

Coach Tim ran up to the reporter and yelled, "No further questions!" He took my arm and started to lead me away. He went behind the home run fence with me, kneeled down on his knee, and looked into my eyes. My parents were following us. "Jimmy, take a deep breath and relax. You're not obligated to speak to anyone right now. Just take some deep breaths so we can figure this out."

All of a sudden, I heard a noise. It sounded like hundreds of bumble bees were swarming in the distance. I looked in the direction of the sound as it got louder and louder. I looked toward the field, but nobody else seemed to hear it. Coach was still kneeling next to me, but he didn't seem to hear the noise either.

In the distance, right where the sound was coming from, I saw an old lady. A man was trying to grab her purse from her. But it wasn't just some old lady. It was Anthony's Grandma! I took a baseball from the ground and threw it at the robber. The eczema-covered baseball hit the robber right in the chest. Instantly, the robber was covered with white webs. It must have been eczema webs. The robber couldn't move his arms or legs, no matter how hard he tried. In fact, after a few minutes, he looked like he stopped trying. He wasn't moving at all. He looked frozen. Completely frozen in place! He slid down to the ground.

Before I could turn around to look back toward the baseball field, police officers were walking toward me. My heart started to race. I felt the pounding in my chest, and I started to feel lightheaded. They were going to arrest me for what I did - I was sure of it. I was in big trouble.

But they walked right past me, picked up the robber, and carried him into their police car. I could breath! What a relief.

Suddenly another truck pulled up to the field. It said BIA on its side. The Brain Intelligence Agency was here. Are you kidding me? Were they the ones who were going to take me away? Did they think I helped rob Anthony's Grandma? Was I being arrested for the eczema pitch?

I tried to run, but in two seconds I was already being led to the truck by two men in dark suits. My parents quickly followed us and convinced the two men to let them go in the van with me so I wasn't alone. Before I could even turn around, the two men in the dark suits disappeared, and there was a different big, strong man in the truck. He looked right at me with a very serious expression on his face.

"Jimmy, my name is Andrew. I work for the BIA and will be taking you for a couple of small tests."

The truck had no windows, and there were a lot of computers inside of it. I couldn't see who was driving because there was a solid white wall between the back of the van and the front. Andrew took my blood pressure and all of my measurements (my height and weight) and drew blood from a vein in my right hand. It hurt for a second, but then I was okay. "Where are we going?" asked my mom nervously.

Andrew responded that he couldn't tell us. "The location is secret government information."

We rode in silence for a really long time - it seemed like hours - until the van suddenly stopped. I knew we must have arrived. My mom took my hand and walked me into the secret location. I saw a lot of angles on the building, and it was very big. Tall that is. Then Andrew announced, "Welcome to the Octagon."

I found out the Octagon is a building the government uses to perform all types of secret tests and investigations. You can't even get in if you don't have something called clearance, meaning my family and I had to have special permission to enter. The name Octagon comes from the shape of the building. It has eight sides. The best part about entering the Octagon was how important it made me feel. But I have to admit, something inside was really bothering me. I was worried about Randy, my catcher, and whether he would be okay.

When we got inside, I was amazed by everything I saw. Hundreds of scientists were walking around in long white lab coats, and lots of secret service members were planted in locations throughout the building. I could tell by the earpieces in their ears. I turned around to find Andrew, but he was gone.

Wait a minute. If there are secret service members, then where is the man whom they protect? Within minutes of asking myself that question, the President showed up.

"Hi Jimmy" said President Jenkins. President Jenkins used to be a Senator from my home state of Maryland. He was always nice on television. And to my understanding, he also was nice in person. He seemed nice right now.

I had no clue what to do for such a high-class man. I saluted him and said, "Hello Sir."

He laughed and said there's no need to salute him. He started to talk to my parents while walking us down a long hallway. "Jimmy, don't be scared. I'm taking you to our main lab so the government can do some tests."

The entrance to the lab was like a bullpen at a baseball stadium. We walked through the entrance, which was long and narrow, and we entered what looked like a very strange baseball diamond. It was designed in red, white, and blue. The turf field was blue, the bases were red, and the pitcher's mound in the center was white. This definitely was not the way I pictured a laboratory. There were no tables, no chairs, no flasks, and no solutions in jars or test tubes.

A grown man who resembled a catcher was standing on a red home plate. He was wearing a facemask, shoulder pads, kneepads, a chest plate, and all of the other catcher's equipment. There were other grown adults on first, second, and third bases. They also were dressed like baseball players. They were wearing red, white, and blue USA Jerseys and white baseball pants, and each had a baseball glove on one hand.

It was very strange. It was just my parents, the players, President Jenkins, and me in this room that had a red, white, and blue baseball diamond. How could this be a lab? It was all very confusing.

I was surprised when out of nowhere a tall woman in glasses and a long white coat with a clipboard in her hand came out of a door that was camouflaged into a white wall. I didn't even see the doorknob on the wall. She walked up to the pitcher's mound, bent down, and picked up something I recognized. She had grabbed a speed gun. I used one all of the time with my dad to see how fast I could pitch.

President Jenkins (I was still super surprised to see him, by the way) tapped my back, handed me a baseball, and said "Jimmy, do your thing."

I took the ball, walked over to the mound, and fired it at home plate as hard and fast as I could. I knew the speed gun was measuring my speed, and I knew I was pitching in front of the President of the United States. I definitely had to throw a strike. As the ball left my hand, eczema flew off my hand with the ball. The ball was completely covered in eczema by the time it reached home plate.

"Ninety-six miles per hour," shouted the catcher. I actually wasn't even concerned with the eczema. To be honest, I cared more about my pitch. That was the fastest I had ever thrown! I was only twelve years old and just threw a ninety-six mile per hour ball. Before that, I had never thrown faster than sixty miles per hour.

The scientists also were impressed. "Wow! World Record for your age!" exclaimed the first baseman.

Now we're talking! This was fun! I looked at the woman in the long white coat, the one who entered the field from the mysterious door. She was taking lots and lots of notes and scribbling loads of information onto her clipboard. She kept looking at me, at the catcher, at the ball in the catcher's hand, and back at her clipboard. And the entire time, she didn't stop taking notes.

I felt a little bad for the poor catcher. I know he was covered in equipment, but there definitely was a clear side effect to anyone who caught my pitches. They got covered with eczema. The catcher had it all over his cleats, his jersey, his kneepads, and even his mask. He looked like a mummy. I wanted to laugh, but nobody else was laughing. So I didn't.

The catcher held the ball in his glove, walked over to the woman in the long white coat, and placed the ball in what looked like a clear square lucite box. As he put the ball into the box, some eczema oozed off of his glove.

As I was watching the exchange of the ball into the lucite box, two men walked out of the bullpen carrying a person on a stretcher. The men holding the stretcher each had on turquoise scrubs, and masks covered their faces. They curiously walked over to the woman in the long white coat and whispered for a while. Again, the woman in the long white coat looked at me, looked at the catcher, looked at the person on the stretcher, and wrote notes for what seemed like forever. She then looked at my parents who were standing in the corner of the bullpen. They both looked frightened and puzzled. This was all happening so quickly, and nobody was sharing any information with us. What was going on? Why was someone here on a stretcher?

As the men carrying the stretcher walked toward the camouflaged white door, I caught a glimpse of the patient. It was Randy, my baseball team's catcher. He wasn't moving. He was covered in white eczema. It looked like spider webs. He was silent. He wasn't even breathing. At least, I didn't think he was. My heart started to pound in my chest.

The woman in the long white coat looked at me. She must have realized I was really, really scared. "He's alive. Don't worry. He's just completely frozen. We need to perform some tests on him."

Now this was getting scary. I was afraid to move. Nobody moved. I think they were all thinking what I was thinking as we looked toward the catcher on the red, white and blue laboratory field. Was this catcher, the scientist catcher, going to freeze also? We all just waited and watched silently. It seemed so long. The woman in the long white coat just stared at the catcher and scribbled notes nonstop. And then it happened. The scientist catcher started to move in slow motion and then suddenly froze in place.

Two minutes later, three men in turquoise scrubs and masks walked onto the field out of the camouflaged door. "The eczema ball froze some of the cells in Randy's body," one of them stated aloud. "Our initial tests reveal the eczema balls only freeze cells for one hour, and the person who is frozen is put in a state of sleep. Then you can peel the eczema harmlessly off of the body."

"Enough time for the police to get the crook, and take him to jail!" exclaimed President Jenkins with excitement.

"Jimmy has had a lot of surprises today. Do you think he will be able to rest soon please?" asked my dad.

"Absolutely," replied President Jenkins before escorting me off the field toward the bullpen. When we reached the bullpen, he whispered something into my ear I couldn't believe. I didn't understand what he meant. I didn't want to do it. Did I have to do it?

"Jimmy," he said, "you will need to start a new life."

HOLD UP!

A new life? Does he mean a new identity or stop being a normal kid? This is all moving so quickly. But can we just talk about the fact that this day is INSANE! My eczema has bothered me my entire life. And now not only have I lost my eczema, but I have met the President of the United States, set a world record, and somehow have a superpower!!! This is all crazy! I can't wait to speak with my friends about it!

CHAPTER 3

A NEW (BUT HARD) LIFE

*T*he President and a group of scientists sat down with my parents at a round table they set up in the corner of the room as another scientist measured the length of my arms and fingers. So odd! I couldn't make out exactly what the adults were whispering at the table, but I could make out some of the words here and there. Crime. Responsibilities. Help us on the streets. Promise to keep him safe. **What were they talking about?**

I soon found out. The scientist finished my measurements and walked me over to the table where the adults had been speaking. My mom seemed worried. I knew by the way she was looking at me – her eyes looked watery, and her lips were pressed tightly together. My dad put his arm around me. I found out my new responsibilities as soon as I sat down. They would include daily training, conditioning, fighting crime, and learning all of the locations on the map. I could spend time with my family, but I had to be sure to set aside time to handle all of my new responsibilities. I asked if I could finish the baseball season. President Jenkins looked at me with a very serious expression on his face. "Sorry Jimmy. Your pitches release powerful eczema that is too dangerous."

Before this eczema power, baseball was my life. I ate, breathed, and dreamed baseball. I watched baseball on television, traded baseball cards with my buddies, and tried to go to every stadium I could with my dad. President Jenkins's words burned me; I felt like crying.

His next words stung me even more. "Unfortunately, the entire baseball season for the whole league is over until further notice."

I ran toward a bench in the lab bullpen and put my head down. I couldn't swallow without a pain in my throat. I told my dad that I wanted to go home. My eyes were filled up with tears. I couldn't even think straight. I drove home in a van with President Jenkins, angry and sad, not even paying attention when President Jenkins was explaining my new life to my parents. Baseball was literally all my friends and I talked about. We couldn't stop playing. If the league was shut down, that meant one hundred baseball players – nine teams - would have to stop playing! And right before the biggest game of our season!

The whole ride home I thought about my friends. Would I ever see them again? Would I even get to talk to them? Are they all going to be so angry with me for ruining the season? It wasn't fair. I didn't choose for this to happen; why was I being punished? It was bad enough that I was the only one of my friends who had this awful eczema. Now this! I would just say no. I just wanted to be myself again and my old life back! Could I say no?

I told the President that all I wanted was to still be able to see my friends. He didn't know what to say at first. He put his hand on my shoulder. "Jimmy, people can't know about all of the government secrets that you will know. They can't know the locations of your training. But you are going to witness some spectacular things that people don't usually get to see."

I had no idea what he meant. What plans? What training? What was going on?

President Jenkins told my parents they would need to take me to the store to buy me a cell phone that the government would set up for me.

Cool! I had never had my own cell phone. This was starting to sound a lot better. The President told me that for the first few days, this was the only way I could communicate with my friends. I couldn't see them, but I could speak with them.

He then explained to my parents and me the big plans. He and the whole government had huge plans for me. My parents kept looking at each other. My mom looked scared. My dad put his arm around her to try to relax her, but he looked scared too. Could they say no to President Jenkins?

HOLD UP!

Don't get me wrong. I was scared also, and I didn't want my life to change. But after hearing the plans – I will be totally honest with you. I started to get really, really, really excited. I was about to get my very own cell phone!!!!!!! I couldn't sleep the entire night.

The next day my parents took me to the phone store, and a secret service agent met us at the door as soon as we entered. He told me to pick out any phone I wanted. It was on the house. FREE!

I was so happy. I ran around the store looking at every phone. New phones, old phones, even tablets. I finally found the new G-Phone 15. The one in all of the new commercials. It was purple and black. I always liked Ravens colors. The secret service escort started to set it up for me. First, I created an email address. Then, I put Anthony's email into my contacts. I wrote to him right away . . . "Guess what I just got!"

He didn't care about me getting the phone. He cared about what happened yesterday. "Jimbo, where are you? What happened at the game? Are you okay? Are you sick? Was that eczema on the ball?"

I knew I wasn't allowed to answer some of his questions. I told him I was okay, nothing was wrong, and I promised I would call him later. I had other stuff on my mind. This phone was awesome! I had only had a computer before. It was not as updated as a phone. The phone had games, internet, calling, texting, and a virtual assistant named Sophie. "Try talking to Sophie," said my mom.

"What is your favorite baseball team Sophie?" I asked. I was almost scared for the answer. My phone was about to talk to me! Then Sophie responded, "I am not super into sports, though the web says that the New York Yellow Jackets have won 27 championships." I didn't love that answer because I was always a huge Maryland Mongoose fan, but it made sense!

When I got home, I called Anthony and tried to explain everything. But I couldn't tell him most of the details because I wasn't allowed to speak about my training or the cool training locations. I told him about the relief I felt in my hands from the itching and burning as soon as I threw the eczema pitch. I told him I had to be checked out by doctors and scientists after I left the field to try to understand what happened. I laughed with him about Randy being covered in eczema. Gross! Anthony told me all about people's reactions. It felt like we were on the phone for twenty minutes, though we actually were on the phone for two hours. Time really flew by.

I couldn't sleep that entire night again. I was scared, excited, and anxious for the following day. My head kept replaying every detail from the past two days in my mind. I think I finally fell asleep around four in the morning. Before I realized it, my mom came into my room to say it was eight o'clock and time to wake up to start the day.

My mom and I were supposed to arrive at the Octagon by noon for my first day of training. On the way, we stopped at the ice cream parlor. ICE CREAM FOR BREAKFAST! WOOHOO! I asked the man at the counter for a vanilla ice cream cone with sprinkles. When I tried to take it from the counter, the way my hand was spread out must have been a trigger for my eczema. Eczema shot out of my right hand toward the ice cream machine. Everyone in the store went crazy; some shouted, and others ran out the door. People moved as far as they could away from me. I tried to stay calm. I tried to understand that when people first saw my power, they wouldn't know what to do and might get scared of me. But the more that people gave me funny looks, the more I felt very sad.

Would people ever like me again, or would they think I'm a monster? I took my ice cream and ran out to the car. I couldn't stand seeing everyone's reactions to me. I wondered if my life would be like that forever.

My mom drove us to the Octagon in a silent car. I didn't have any interest in eating my ice cream. When we arrived at the science lab, I told the scientists that I wanted to control my power. All they said is that I would receive training for that.

"In fact," said one of the scientists, "you are about to start that training right now." He handed me a white envelope that was sealed with a picture of the American eagle on it. I opened it carefully and read it.

Training Day 1: Control and Take Down

Hi Jimmy. Your first challenge is to take down all of the crooks. Avoid hitting pedestrians! During this activity, cardboard pop ups (with pictures of children or robbers on them) will randomly appear out of nowhere. Your job is to eczema the robbers. You will be set up in the middle of the room. There is a bucket of baseballs next to where you will be standing. Say"Ready" when you want to start. Good Luck!

Okay. Sounded easy . . . Take down the crooks. I can do that. I grabbed a couple of baseballs and yelled "READY."

I waited a couple of seconds, but nothing happened. I yelled again "Rea…"

Then I saw it out of the corner of my left eye - a pop up of a robber carrying a bag full of money. I threw a baseball directly at him; the ball immediately was plastered in eczema the second I released it from my fingertips. The pop up figure froze in front of me in a cube of eczema. Before I could even react with shock, I heard another pop up behind me. I threw the ball as quickly as I could without looking. I didn't even turn. It was so strange. I never would have tried to throw like that before. I had a newfound confidence. Without even turning, I had reached my right arm around my back and released the ball. A backhanded pitch.

"Try again," said a loud computer voice. I could have sworn I heard the eczema ball hit the pop up. It was a loud crashing noise. I was confused until I turned around. Behind me was a completely frozen eczema-covered pop up of a child licking a lollipop. Over and over again, the scientists made me do that exercise until I could distinguish between the good guys and bad guys. Robber. Child. Robber. Robber. Child. Robber. Child. Child.

At first, I kept throwing the eczema balls at every pop up. But after about thirty throws, I somehow figured out how to distinguish the robbers from everyone else. I somehow got this feeling that told me when to throw an eczema ball and when not to throw one.

I also was starting to sense the exact moment the eczema would release from my fingertips during my throws. My throw was one fluid motion, but there was a specific tingling sensation right before the eczema would exit my fingertips. I kept thinking about the ice cream incident and knew I now would be able to control that release.

Two hours after I started, I ran out of baseballs. My right arm was so sore from pitching, and my brain was getting tired. I asked for a water break, but President Jenkins said I had completed training for the day. I had worked so hard for hours.

"I have a special surprise for you, Jimmy," he told me. Then the most amazing thing ever happened.

CHAPTER 4
THE MOST AMAZING THING

We walked down a new long, narrow corridor I hadn't seen before. There were photos on the walls of former Presidents in big gold frames. At the end of the hall was a single dark blue door. President Jenkins reached for the handle and turned his head toward me with a big smile on his face. He turned the knob, and as he pushed the door open, white fog filled the entranceway. I felt a rush of cold air and looked into a room that seemed to be filled with puffy white clouds. I followed President Jenkins with my parents by my side. We each used our hands to push the clouds out of the way, as if we were swimming the breaststroke through the clouds. We swam and swam until the room suddenly became clearer. The fog had disappeared, and a single bright white light shined down from the ceiling onto a red and yellow suit that was somehow floating in midair. No strings were attached to it, and no mannequin was wearing it. It was just floating in the air like a ghost in a movie.

The front of the suit was really cool. It was made of a stretchy bright red shirt and shiny yellow spandex pants. The red shirt had a logo in the center of it – a large baseball glove with a baseball directly in the center of it. White lines were crisscrossed all over the baseball. They looked like cobwebs. The cobwebs were supposed to be my eczema! I asked why the suit was there. Two scientists had just entered the room. One of them exclaimed, "What superhero doesn't have a supersuit!"

"Well, Jimmy hasn't had one . . . until now!" responded the second scientist.

"YES!!!" I shouted as loud as I could. It was the coolest, most awesome supersuit ever. It was sick! The red shirt was as bright and shiny as a brand new fire truck, and the metallic yellow pants had pockets all the way up and down the legs. I could put my new phone in one!

"We may have to make some adjustments," said the first scientist. "So we need you to try it on for size."

Are you kidding me? This was crazy. The scientist reached toward the suit and pulled it out of the thin air. I looked to see if any strings were holding it up, but there were none. I still couldn't figure out how they got it to float in the air. Did that mean I would float in it when I wore it?

The female scientist handed it to me and pointed me toward a dressing room. As I went to put on my new suit, I noticed there was huge black print on the back of the shirt.

ECZEMA MAN. I could barely breath from happiness. Was that me? Eczema Man?

The suit fit perfectly. I could barely control my excitement. I felt like screaming and calling all of my friends. But then I was reminded there was work to be done. The second scientist told me that I needed to return home to learn about my new responsibilities. I turned toward President Jenkins to thank him and ask him if I would need to take the suit with me, but he was gone. I hadn't even seen him leave. I looked further behind me to see if he was there, but all I could see was fog. He definitely was gone. Nobody mentioned his disappearance, so neither did I. The scientists told me I should leave the suit at the laboratory for them to make some special adjustments to it.

When my mom and I arrived at my house, I practically skipped through the front door. As soon as I entered the living room, there were lots of people in navy suits standing in the room. Sitting on the sofa was President Jenkins.

How was that even possible! President Jenkins was talking to my dad, who was sitting right next to him. I overheard them speaking. "First and foremost, he needs to know that fighting crime is not about fame. It's about getting the job done and helping society."

My stomach started to feel queasy. That's a lot of responsibility. I knew what the President was trying to say. A superhero really needs to take the job seriously. President Jenkins turned toward me.

"Hi Jimmy. I was just explaining to your father how important your job is. It's not for fame or popularity. You are now serving a larger cause – you are helping the world. Come sit next to me Jimmy," and he patted the sofa cushion next to him.

"Second, training is very, very important. I heard about what happened at the ice cream parlor earlier today, and I'm sorry. It might happen a lot. People don't understand your ability. You need to learn your strengths and weaknesses. You have to be in complete control of every thought you have and every single move you make."

I shook my head, wondering how long it would take me to do that and if it was even possible.

"You see Jimmy, that's why we had you practice take down and control techniques today." The President turned toward my mother. "Beth, do you still have the paper with Jimmy's assignment on it?" (Beth is my mom's name). She told him she did and took it out of her purse, the purple one my family bought her for her 40th birthday. She handed the paper to President Jenkins, who examined the assignment.

"My staff created this – they're the best," said President Jenkins. "And this is a very good way to practice control. But I might have an even better way. Let's go outside and shoot your eczema with your left hand at the tall tree in your backyard."

I had never ever thrown a baseball with my left hand, especially an eczema ball. I have always been a righty (though I would love to be a southpaw to have a better chance to make the big leagues). A secret service man handed me a baseball, the President wished me good luck, and I walked outside. Everyone was advised to stay inside just in case something happened that could harm anyone. I took the baseball, got into my stance and threw. The ball didn't even travel twenty feet. How embarrassing! It wasn't covered in eczema either. My left hand just wasn't strong enough. For so many years, my right hand helped me dominate on the pitcher's mound. My dad had spent hours and hours with me, practicing my pitches with my right hand. Batting cages. Baseball fields. Little league games. Travel teams. That's why that very first eczema ball I ever threw had such tremendous power. I threw it with all of my might – WITH MY RIGHT HAND.

President Jenkins shouted through the window for me to try it again. Though I thought it was useless, this time I really, really focused. I needed to match the strength and placement of my right-handed pitches. I firmly dug my foot into the dirt, wound up, and threw the pearl with all of my might. This one had to work! I had given it all I had.

But it didn't. It traveled about 30mph and only went about five feet further than my previous pitch. I looked toward the den window, and I felt a large lump in my throat. It was hard to swallow. Maybe this was all just a bad idea. I just wanted to be normal again. This wasn't going to work.

Then President Jenkins said the worst words I had heard him say so far. "The only way to teach your left hand and your brain to work together is through muscle memory. In

CHAPTER 5

FROM BEST TO WORST: AMBIDEXTROUS

I heard him, but I didn't like it. The worst word ever! Ambidextrous. I said I would LIKE to be a southpaw. But I could barely write my name with my left hand. Now I would have to use it to do everything! I didn't want to be disrespectful, but I couldn't control my feelings.

"WHAT!" I shouted. "That will take weeks."

"Or will it?" asked President Jenkins. "You now will have access to the best technology. We've been working for years on a device that has capabilities you wouldn't believe. It's called the IG2, and it can train your non-dominant hand to imitate the capabilities of your dominant hand. We already measured the exact movements, patterns and angles you use with your right hand, your dominant hand. Now the IG2 will help your left hand duplicate the motions of your right hand by training your brain to work together with your muscle memory to make your left hand stronger and more controlled."

"That's incredible!"

"Well Jimmy. We hope to do some really incredible things with this technology someday. We hope to help children learn to write. Maybe we can use it to improve the capabilities of older people who have unsteady hands as they age. We hope to help people who have lost the use of parts of their bodies. The opportunities are end-less. People who can't walk may someday be able to walk again. For now, we're still in the preliminary stages. But we have high expectations and big dreams, and we're go-ing to try it on you."

I couldn't wait to see this invention. "Where is it?" I asked.

"It's at the Octagon; we will introduce it to you first thing in the morning at 9am."

"That's pretty far from where we live in Maryland. It's a three-hour drive in rush hour traffic. To be there by 9am tomorrow morning, we would have to leave here by 6am," my mom responded concerned.

"No problem," replied the President. "You're helping your country, Jimmy. Beth, leave the worrying to me. My private jet makes it a 20 minute flight."

My mom and I looked at each other, and I knew we were thinking the same thing. My eyes welled up, and my throat started to hurt.

"President," said my mom, "that may be a challenge." Then she was quiet. Very quiet. She looked at me, expecting me to speak, but I didn't. She looked at me again.

"Jimmy has a huge phobia of flying."

I was so embarrassed. Why did she tell him? My mom just told the President of the United States one of my biggest secrets. Not even Anthony knew! And now President Jenkins will think I'm too weak to become a superhero.

I felt my face turn bright red. I couldn't be there. I walked away and rushed upstairs as fast as I could. I knew my mom was going to tell the story to the President. The most upsetting story ever!

I heard my mom as I shut the door. "A couple of years ago, our family was flying to California. As you know, Jimmy loves baseball. So did Benny Jaxon, our neighbor's son. Jimmy and Benny had played little league together for years. Our families decided to surprise the boys for their seventh birthdays by taking them together on a trip to watch some baseball games in California. The Angels. The Dodgers. The Athletics. The Padres. The Giants. We had saved up for tickets for ages, and we had planned the trip for months. The boys were so excited. Benny had never flown on an airplane, so it was an especially big deal. It was going to be such a special trip."

My mom paused. I knew what she was feeling. It had been a long time, but I'll never forget it. Neither would she.

My mom continued, "We found out later that Benny had an ear infection. But at the time, we didn't know. During the flight to California, Benny was crying. Actually he was screaming in pain. He kept saying his ears were hurting. It was a really long flight, and nothing any of us did made the pain go away. We gave him chewing gum and lollipops. We tried to teach him to pop his ears. Nothing worked. He just kept crying. We felt awful for him."

My mom paused. "When we finally landed in Pasadena, we darted to baggage claim. Benny was still crying and holding his ears. The man who was sitting behind us on the plane started to walk toward Martin, Benny's father. We thought he was going to see if Benny was feeling better. Instead, he started to scream and yell, 'You have a lot of nerve taking a crying child on a plane like that. I had to sit there for hours listening to that brat scream because you couldn't shut him up!' He pointed at Benny and screamed even louder, 'You robbed me! You robbed me of a peaceful flight to California. Now you'll see what it feels like to be robbed!' Then he grabbed Benny and ran as fast as he could. Martin ran and ran after the man, screaming for him to stop. We all started to run after them and yell for help. But we were outrun. The police have been trying to help us find Benny since that day. It turns out the man who took Benny was a crazy man who had been to jail seven times. So he was a pro with getting away. We still haven't found him. But I know Benny's ok. I just feel it. For days, the police asked us lots of questions. We described the man. We told them everything he said. The police asked if we noticed anything unusual about him. All we could tell the police was that the man had a tattoo on his wrist shaped like the state of Maryland, he had a goatee, and he was wearing a vest that read Becket Pioneers."

HOLD UP!

With all of the thoughts going through my mind about Benny, I closed my door to drown out the sound of my mom telling the story. It was the worst vacation we ever took, and I wish we never flew on that airplane. The more I thought about that trip and that awful flight, the more upset I got. I rushed out of my room, ran down the steps, threw open the backyard door and ran outside as quickly as I could. I picked up a baseball from the ground with my left hand, and I threw it toward the tree as hard as I could. I was so angry. All of the pressure of the last few days hit me. The memories of the flight and that trip came back to me. I threw that ball toward that tree so hard that my left hand actually hurt. It wasn't as strong as my right hand, but I did it. I threw the ball with my left hand!

My mom walked outside to speak with me. "This must be very hard for you."

"I miss Benny, and I just want to be normal again. I want to hang out with Anthony or at least speak more to him. I'm not a normal kid anymore. Anthony doesn't even know why I've barely called him. He probably thinks I'm angry with him or maybe he's upset with me." I started to cry even more.

"Then you should call him."

I needed to speak with Anthony. He picked up on the first ring. As soon as I said hello, Anthony could tell something was wrong. "Are you okay?"

I told him as much as I could. I didn't tell him about the suit or the training or the laboratory. I didn't tell him about the IG2 or the muscle memory technology. I told him I missed Benny. I told him I missed playing baseball outside and our homemade homerun derbies where we tried to see who could hit a whiffle ball further over my neighbor Ali's fence.

Anthony asked if I could play outside. Every day after school that's what we did since I could remember. I didn't know if I was allowed. But didn't President Jenkins say I still needed to live a normal life as long as I kept top secrets private?

I went inside and asked if I could spend some time with Anthony. "Sure Jimmy. It's been a long few days. Go have some fun with your friend."

President Jenkins was a really nice guy.

Anthony invited some other friends over. Cameron, Brooke, and Lucas. I missed them. We played soccer for four hours! It was so fun, and I had the best time. When my mom called me in for dinner, I couldn't believe how long we had been outside.

"Would your friends like to join us for spaghetti and meatballs? Your favorite! We definitely have enough," my mom shouted.

We were all starving, and we ate dinner so quickly. We talked about how crazy the past few days had been. I think they could tell I had been stressed, or maybe Anthony suggested they not bring up too much about my eczema. Anthony knew me so well. Instead, we told old stories about funny things we all did together. We laughed about the time Anthony's dog Maggie jumped into a mud puddle right after we all gave her a bath. We talked about the time we were going to the school carnival in Lucas's mom's car and got a flat tire. Brooke reminded us of the time we all raked up leaves in my backyard into the highest piles ever and jumped into them over and over again.

What a great night. I felt better when I went to sleep that night. I decided it was time to overcome my fear. I was going to Washington, DC, on the jet with my parents the next morning. That's what Benny would want me to do. Maybe I could use my superhero powers to find him. And I really wanted to see that machine!

Scientists were waiting for my family and me when we arrived. Right away, they asked me to throw a baseball toward a net . . . with my left hand! I knew I could do it. I did it the day before. I wound up with as much power as I could and pitched it the way I did toward the tree at my house. The throw was okay but definitely not as accurate as I would have liked. They recorded the speed and distance of my throw. Then they asked me to write my name on a piece of notebook paper . . . with my left hand. What a mess. It definitely did not look like my name at all. One of the scientists placed the notebook paper in a clear case. Then they walked me over to a long wooden table.

There was a block shaped like a rectangle in the middle of the table with an object sitting on top of it. It was obvious I was staring at the IG2. It looked like a long gray sleeve with a glove attached to the end of it. But the glove wasn't a baseball glove. It looked like a gold latex glove, just not as thin as a latex glove. It kept its shape, probably so my fingers could easily slide into it. Two silver Velcro bands were loosely wrapped around the sleeve that was connected to this glove. I knew I was going to have to slide my left hand into the glove and was scared. Everybody was watching me silently, as if I was supposed to know what to do.

I looked at them and walked toward it. One of the scientists shook his head and motioned toward it. I slowly slid the fingers of my left hand into the IG2. As soon as the tips of my fingers reached the end of the glove, the glove started to tighten around my fingertips. It got tighter and tighter until I could barely tell where my fingers ended and the glove started. It was almost as if the glove molded to my hand. Then without me even doing anything and without the scientists touching anything, the Velcro straps automatically adjusted the sleeve around my arm so that the sleeve was wrapped as tightly as it could be around my left arm.

I was then asked to repeat the same things I did before the IG2 was on me. First I had to throw the baseball as hard as I could toward the net. It was a little hard with the IG2 wrapped so tightly around my left arm, but I tried my best to place the ball into the center of the net at full speed. I still wasn't happy with my accuracy. The same scientist as before asked me to write my name with my left hand on a piece of notebook paper again. I did that too. It wasn't very neat. You could barely tell it was my name.

One of the scientists walked over to me with a laptop in his arms. He started to press loads of buttons on his computer. He kept looking at the IG2 on my arm and pressing more buttons.

Then the craziest thing happened. The IG2 started to shift around on my arm. My fingers wiggled on their own; the Velcro straps loosened and tightened in different spots; and I felt a warm sensation in my fingertips. I just stood there for a few minutes as all of this happened, not knowing what to do. I looked down at the glove, watching it move around. Then suddenly, with no warning, the Velcro straps automatically loosened, and the pressure around my fingers disappeared. The IG2 became loose on me. A scientist came over and slid the IG2 off of my left arm. It felt so good to be relieved from the pressure.

One of the scientists placed the IG2 back onto the block on the wooden table. She then handed me a baseball and asked me to throw it into the net WITH MY LEFT HAND.

I'm not sure why. It didn't seem like the IG2 helped me very much.

I got into my stance and threw the baseball. It went directly into the center of the net - as fast as I had ever thrown it and 100 feet! When the scientist asked me to write my name in cursive on a piece of notebook paper, it was perfect! I jumped with happiness. In a couple of minutes, I became better at things that would have taken years of work. All with my left hand! How was that even possible? President Jenkins smiled at me. I smiled back. So sick!

I knew the scientists were writing down the speed and accuracy of my pitches. I knew they were taking notes on my coordination. But I didn't know something else they had been watching until they told me. No matter how hard I pitched the ball with my left hand, even when it was as fast as my right-handed pitch, I never once threw an eczema ball. They told me that's what they had been hoping for. I would now work on strengthening my left hand so I could perform different tasks with my left hand without eczema shooting out. Every day I would need to tape up my right hand for three hours and only use my left hand for everything I did. Everything.

I had to start right then. The same scientist who had been pressing buttons on a laptop wrapped my right hand in tape, and we played lots of fun games with me using my left hand. Board games. Ping pong. Pool. Air hockey. At first it was very hard for me to get used to using my left hand. The scientist told me that with practice, it would get easier. He said it would only take a few days.

CHAPTER 6

THE COOLEST WAY TO TRAVEL

*T*he next morning, President Jenkins came to my house. My right hand was wrapped up, and the President told me I should take it off. "Jimmy, it's time to put on your suit. It's time to start."

It sounded official. Important. But it was way too soon!

My heart started to beat really hard and really quickly. I don't know if I was excited or scared or both. I took the suit from President Jenkins and went into the bathroom. The suit was shiny and silky, and the color red was so bright. I slid into it, and all of a sudden, I felt more confident with it on. I put my arms on my hips, looked into the mirror, held my head up high, and just couldn't stop looking.

I stepped outside of the bathroom feeling more heroic than I had ever felt in my life. I loved the smile on my mom's face when she saw me. Her eyes got really wide.

"I love it! So cool!" my mom announced. "Get comfy," she said. "President Jenkins says you will be wearing it a lot."

My father was beaming with pride; I could tell he was really happy for me.

It was Training Day Number 2. I wondered what I would be doing.

When we arrived at the Octagon, I was told to go to the usual lab, the one I had been taken to a couple of times before. This time, nobody was there, but there was a note waiting for me about that day's training.

Training Day 2: Travel

Hi Jimmy. When you are fighting crime, you will be going from city to city. You can't just travel in your mom's minivan. In today's training, you will be learning how to make an eczema force-field ball. To make a force-field ball, you shoot eczema from your right hand and control it with your left hand. It's the same as controlling your handwriting with each hand. First you shoot eczema with your right hand. Then you quickly grab the eczema with your left hand before it can go far. Then spread out the eczema by stretching it as you pull your right and left hands apart like silly putty. Finally, you must stretch out the eczema wide enough for you to step onto the stretched-out eczema. Once you are inside, the force-field ball automatically will close around you so you are inside of it. *RUN! RUN AS FAST AS YOU CAN!* The force-field ball will stretch with you. *It will feel like you are moving at the speed that you are running, but it is really going almost one hundred fifty miles per hour. You should get to any situation within three minutes maximum this way. One last thing, we will be practicing outside today. Good luck!*

HOLD UP!

Are you absolutely kidding me! I'm going to travel in time in a large ball of eczema. How is that even possible? I felt like a superhero in a comic book! That was the coolest, most amazing thing I had ever heard.

I was so excited for the day's training. One hundred fifty miles per hour! I pitched an eczema ball with my right hand and reached out with my left hand to grab it. But grabbing onto it was going to be a problem. My left hand slipped and the momentum and strength of the eczema threw me five feet across the grass. So I got up and tried it again. And again. And again. And again. After lots of tries, I finally grabbed onto it. It was sticky and very hard to stretch. I had no idea the eczema would be so thick. I stretched it apart as much as I could. I got to that point a few times. Finally it became more simple. Eventually stepping onto it became easier. I'm not sure how I didn't stick to the inside of the eczema ball. But I didn't. The inside was not sticky, even though the outside was. Odd.

The hardest part came next. I had to figure out how to stand still and let the eczema close up around me. I kept getting afraid it would stick to me. And what if I didn't move my hands quickly enough when I was holding on to the two sides of it? Would my hands get stuck to the eczema and prevent the ball from closing around me? Would the ball start to travel before I was completely wrapped in it? I soon realized there was nothing to worry about. Somehow, the ball just closed before I even could think about it. It just happened naturally. I would find myself wrapped up in a big ball of eczema – not stuck to the sides, my hands on the inside, and the ball not moving.

How do I start this thing? I asked myself. I thought about the letter. *Just run. Run as fast as you can.* I ran and ran and ran until I hit an invisible fence. I was told that until I learned to stop, which required leaning back slightly onto my left heal while remaining in motion, the invisible fence would prevent me from drifting off too far.

I practiced making eczema force-field balls for four hours. It was so much fun. Once I had it mastered, I was told to study my first lesson again. Control and take down. So I did.

That evening, I was so tired. I was relaxing when Anthony called. "Jimbo Limbo, want to come over tomorrow?"

I couldn't tell him details, but he knew I had training. He was the only person I told. "I can't, I have training," I answered.

"Do you? Aren't you off on weekends?" he asked.

"You're so smart! Yes, I'm off! What time should I come over?"

"12:00. Don't be late though because I have a surprise. See you tomorrow."

Hmmm. I wonder what he meant by that. Hadn't I already had enough surprises for one week! I couldn't sleep.

The next day I went to Anthony's house at 12:00. "Surprise! We are going to the Maryland Mongoose game!" Anthony announced. The Maryland Mongoose is my favorite team. We talked about the game the whole car ride. It felt so good to hang out with Anthony.

We bought our usual hot dogs and popcorn, with lemonade of course, and went to our seats. They were the best seats we ever had. Right on top of the home team dugout! What a great surprise!

"Welcome to Mongoose Park, home of the Maryland Moooooooongooooooooooose," shouted the announcer. Anthony and I yelled Moooooooongooooooooooose as loud as we could with everyone else around us.

"We are five minutes from game time," continued the announcer, "but first we have a surprise."

Anthony and I sat there waiting to hear the surprise. "We would like to recognize someone who is a very special part of our community," said the announcer. "He is twelve years old, plays travel baseball, and is a true hero."

I looked at Anthony, wondering who the hero was.

"I'm sure you have heard, this hero was pitching in a playoff game when he threw an eczema ball. That day he helped our community by saving a lady who was being robbed. Let's give it up for the first superhuman right here in our own town, Jimmy Mancini!" I looked at Anthony in shock.

"That's the surprise!" shouted Anthony. He was standing and clapping with everyone around me. This was crazy. I didn't know what to do. I looked around. Anthony's parents both said to me, "Go down there, Jimmy! This is for you!"

I ran down from our seats onto the field. I heard thousands of fans cheering. It was awesome. All of a sudden my parents showed up on the field. I couldn't believe they knew about the surprise and didn't tell me!

My dad put his arm around me, and the mayor of our town began to speak. "Ladies and Gentleman, Jimmy has been training for weeks. Soon he will be protecting our city. Thank you Jimmy. Thank you for making us feel safe." He handed me a plaque, a baseball, and a picture autographed by all of my favorite players. I could hear screams and applause. What an amazing day!

When I went back through the dugout to my seat, I got to talk to some of the players. A lot of them fist pumped me and gave me high fives. My very favorite pitcher ever, Adam Hamel, said something to me I had on my mind for the rest of the day. "I heard you really can pitch. If you are ambidextrous, you could pitch with that power as a lefty also!"

Now I knew I had to work on my left-handed pitch for sure. If it worked, I could go back to playing baseball with my team. We could win the championship!

HOLD UP!

Not only was Adam Hamel the best pitcher ever, but he had the best idea ever. Now that I could control my left hand, I could put my right hand in my glove and pitch with my left hand for my team. The IG2 had helped me so much with my left hand. Thank you so much Adam Hamel. I was in the best mood ever now.

CHAPTER 7
BACK TO BASEBALL

When the Mongoose game started, hundreds of people came up to me and wished me good luck. They thanked me. They congratulated me. All I kept saying to them was, "Thank you."

What a day. I even got a toss up baseball after an inning. The Mongoose ended up winning the game 7-5. Right when I got home, I ran upstairs, took my phone out of my pocket, ignored the hundreds of texts, and called President Jenkins. When he answered, I was out of breath. I was so excited; I had run out of my parents' car as soon as we got home to make the phone call. I told him all about the idea of me playing baseball with my left hand. The first thing President Jenkins said was, "Adam Hamel should get a big raise!" We both laughed.

"So that's a yes?" I asked.

"Yes Jimmy," President Jenkins said with happiness in his voice.

"Thank you, Thank you, Thank you!" I exclaimed.

I hung up the phone and ran downstairs as fast as I could. "I CAN PLAY! I CAN PLAY!"

"Yay!" both of my parents said at the same time. "I'll let Coach know," said my dad while he held his cell phone up to his ear. I was so happy.

When Coach found out the news, he called the Commissioner of the League. Ever since the first experience with my eczema, the travel league had been postponed until further notice. The next minute, I got a text from Anthony. "Game on tomorrow!!!"

Word sure traveled fast! My father had just been walking into my room to tell me the same thing. I got out my baseball uniform and called coach. "Hey Coach."

"If it isn't my starting LEFT HANDED pitcher. How are you doing?" I didn't answer the question. I just asked, "Is there going to be a catch up practice?"

"Only games," was his answer. "Sorry," he said.

"Alright, see you at the game Coach," I said as I hung up. I was hoping for that answer. But I still wanted to practice with Anthony and my dad. I was a little nervous to use my left hand, and I was even more nervous that eczema might shoot out of it. But the scientists guaranteed me there would be no eczema from my left hand. They had tested it out very thoroughly.

Late that evening, I threw around the ball with my dad for about an hour. Then Anthony came over. We took turns pitching to my dad, fielding grounders, and practicing rundowns. There had never been a rundown in our league, but they were really fun to practice. We ended off practice with fifty sit-ups and some batting practice.

Before I knew it, I was waking up to the biggest day of the year. The league had decided that the two teams with the best records would be playing this game, the finals to the longest baseball season ever. We were playing against the undefeated Lincoln Rams. My mom and dad were so excited. They were wearing baseball caps with our team's name on it. The Wellwood Warriors. It even had a picture of a Wellwood knight with a sword on it. I soon realized every team parent had one on.

The stands were packed with people. People were even lined up outside the fence to watch. Before the game, I had people asking for my autograph. At first I had no clue why. Then one of them asked if I could sign it "Eczema Man." That's when it hit me. I was Eczema Man. I used my left hand to write in cursive just like my Grandma taught me.

Warm ups started. And all of a sudden I heard the umpire shout, "Play ball!" I thought I would be nervous. But I actually was too happy to be nervous. I threw in the first pitch. A strike swinging. I pitched my heart out for four innings. In the fifth inning, I walked two batters. They advanced on a sacrifice bunt. The score was 3-0 at that time. Our center fielder, Rodney, hit a three run homer. I took a look into the stands and saw hundreds of people there. Suddenly, the pressure got to me. I threw a wild pitch that got the man on third home. 3-1. The pitch was hit by their batter and got the other man home. I took a deep breath and refocused. I needed my mind back into the game.

I threw two straight strikeouts to get our team out of the inning. The next inning went quickly with zero hits for either team. Coach took me out and put in Anthony for the last inning. I stood on third as Anthony threw two pitches that were both hit by the Rams' first and second basemen. Both went right to Cameron at second base.

"One more for the title," I heard Cameron shout. Now everyone was pumped up. The next pitch was a double by the pitcher of the Rams. Their pitcher got to third on a single by the next hitter. The man on first stole second as a signal for the man on third to get home to tie the game.

Anthony faked a throw to second and turned to the man on third. He was turning back. "Rundown!" Cameron shouted.

We had been practicing this all year. Cameron went behind me to back me up in case I missed the ball at third base. It was incredible. Anthony threw it to me, and their pitcher ran back home. Cameron ran to third as I threw the ball home, which is where our catcher Randy then made another fake throw to me. Their player ran back to third, I got the ball, and I tagged him.

IT WORKED! WE WON! I heard cheers and saw tears. My team was going crazy. Anthony jumped on my back. It was great to be back. That whole night I celebrated with everyone on my team. It was amazing!

CHAPTER 8
A SMALL STEP FOR HEROES, A GIANT STEP FOR ME

I hadn't saved anyone from any real criminal since that semifinal baseball game. But this day in particular was different. I woke up early just to go to the supermarket with my mom. You're probably thinking *why would he wake up early just to go to the supermarket with his mom?* Usually I would just stay home because my mom would never let me get the types of food or snacks that I want. She always said it was too unhealthy. But now that the scientists recommended I eat a healthy diet, I was much more interested in picking out what I was going to eat.

When we arrived at the supermarket, my mom gave me twenty-five dollars to buy what I wanted (as long as the food was relatively healthy). I had to call her and let her know the aisle I would be in if I was more than two aisles away from her. This was my favorite supermarket. Wellens. I loved it because it got in the newest packs of baseball cards before anywhere else in town.

I was at the front of the store near the cash registers looking at packs of baseball cards when a strange-looking man entered. He kept looking around with his hands in his pockets. But he wasn't walking toward the aisles. He just kept looking at the doors to the supermarket and back at the register. I heard a soft buzzing noise. There were no machines nearby, and my phone wasn't making a sound. I couldn't figure out the source of the buzzing, but it got louder and louder. Nobody else seemed to notice it.

Suddenly, the odd-looking man pulled out a gun from his right pocket.

"Give me any money you have in your register," he said in a low voice to the young woman at the register. I quietly tiptoed toward the left corner of the store near the fruit section. I grabbed some oranges before the man could see me. My eyes scanned all of the aisles to find my mom. Luckily she was nearby, just about to put some grapes into our shopping cart. I motioned for her to stay quiet. My mom couldn't figure out what I was talking about. But before I could even tell her, BOOM! The walls shook from the loudest noise. The man had shot the gun up at the ceiling.

I had the perfect angle. I took one of the oranges and threw it with my right hand as hard as I could directly at him. As soon as my hand released the orange, eczema covered the piece of fruit, and my eczema ball hit the robber right in the ankle. His gun immediately fell out of his hand. Eczema surrounded his legs so he couldn't move, but he wasn't taken down yet. I threw another eczema ball right at the center of his chest. He was covered in eczema, slid down to the floor, and couldn't move. The cashier called the police immediately.

Two minutes later, the police arrived. My mom started to cry and hugged and kissed me so much. I couldn't believe it worked. I was so happy about my second superhero moment. All of a sudden, people started to chant my name. "Jimmy, Jimmy, Jimmy, Jimmy!"

Literally about five minutes later, I heard a loud scream. It was such a loud scream that it hurt my ears. "Mom, what was that?"

"What?" she asked me.

"That loud scream."

"What loud scream Jimmy? I didn't hear anything."

That's when we both understood. I knew I had to help. "It's ok. Go get them Jimmy! But please be careful! I'll tell the police to follow you," my mom shouted.

I shot out eczema with my right hand and used all of my strength to quickly grab it with my left hand. I had both sides of the eczema force-field ball formed. I then spread out the eczema as well as I could – stretching it until it was wide enough for me to step inside of it. Once inside, the eczema suddenly closed up around me. I ran and ran as fast as I could.

Within seconds, I was at a building a few blocks away from the supermarket. I realized it was the BCFL Company Building. BCFL stood for baseball cards for life. It is where all of my favorite baseball cards were made. A lady was screaming from the fourth floor window of the five-story building. A gigantic fire somehow broke out in the building. I realized the screams were not from a robbery. There was no robber to be shot at with eczema. I needed to save this woman from the fire. There had to be a reason I could hear her screams. I'm sure many other people screamed for different reasons all day, but I only heard her screams. It was a sign. I could hear the screams of people in danger.

I had never dealt with fire in my life. I wasn't even allowed to light a match by myself. I didn't know what to do first. Then I had an idea. There were large rocks on the ground. I didn't have any oranges or baseballs, so I picked up the rocks and threw them with my right hand as hard as I could. I shot eczema balls at every angle and hit every spot where there was fire. The fire was moving, so I kept up with it and moved with it. I was very focused on pitching the eczema balls as hard as I could and motioning my hand at the perfect angle. There wasn't much time before the fire would spread. After a minute or two, the entire building was covered in my webs. Best of all, the fire was out. There must not have been enough oxygen for the fire to keep its strength once it was all trapped in my eczema.

I ran up to the fourth floor and helped the lady out of the building. She kissed me on the cheek to thank me. She was crying and crying and thanking me over and over. "You saved my life. You are a real hero."

Two saves within minutes. WOW! I got home and saw that reporters and photographers were at my house. I signed some autographs and even got on television.

An hour later, I was playing baseball catch with my dad when I saw a picture in the sky. At first, I thought it was a cloud. Then I realized it looked like a ball made out of eczema. My dad looked up also and pointed out that light was coming from behind it. At that moment, my phone rang. It was the police. They said that symbol meant I was needed by the police immediately. When I see it, I should call them, put on my suit, and be sure to fill all of my pants pockets with baseballs.

The police needed my help to stop a man who was stealing cake from the Worldwide Vanilla Cake Factory. It was the fanciest place in town. The cakes were delicious, but it was a very fine restaurant also. My parents took my Grandma there once for her birthday. It was my favorite dessert place in the entire world.

As soon as I arrived, I knew exactly who the thief was. They called him Panda. He was called this for three reasons. First, he was fat. Second, he was not very smart. Third, he ate all day long. He went to jail five times in the last year, but he escaped every time. I had seen him on the news. Every time he escaped, he robbed again.

When I got to the Worldwide Vanilla Cake Factory, I could see Panda through the large glass windows. He was holding a knife toward a group of people he must have commanded to stay in the corner since they were all huddled up together there. Panda grabbed what looked like a strawberry shortcake with lots of whipped cream and shoved it into his mouth. He must have seen me as he turned his head toward the window because he started to stare at me. Right away, I pitched a big ball of eczema toward him. It broke through the window, without even making any glass shatter, and it knocked the knife out of Panda's hand. In fact, the knife lay on the floor covered in webs. I then had an idea, but my aim would have to be perfect. It might not work. But I had to try. If I could enclose the hostages in eczema, they would be safe until I could capture Panda. They would freeze soon after, but at least they would be safe. I made believe I was pitching the best pitch of my life and shot a blast of eczema directly toward the hostages. The plan worked. They were trapped together in webs of eczema.

At that point, it was easy. I was definitely feeling more comfortable with this. I did a full round up and pitched a ball with my right hand directly at Panda. He was trapped. He couldn't move. I knew he would soon be asleep.

I was having a great day. When I left the scene of the crime, all of the police officers thanked me. I tried something that actually worked too. I signed my name for them on a wall in eczema. "Don't screw around with my town," I said before leaving.

I went home. While traveling in my eczema ball, I kept thinking about the same topic. Everything that was broken into had something to do with things I loved. Wellens supermarket was my favorite. I got all of my baseball cards from the BCFL building. And I loved the Worldwide Vanilla Cake Factory. How odd! When I entered my house, I shouted, "Mom, I'm home. I'm safe." But I heard my mom crying. I went into the kitchen to find her, and she was on the phone. She seemed very concerned about something someone was saying to her.

I went up to her and heard a man's voice. It was a very deep voice. I moved closer to see the caller ID or to see if I could recognize the voice, but my mom moved the phone away from me and wouldn't let me see who it was. Then she hung up.

"Are you okay? Who was that man?" I asked her.

"Nothing is wrong. I just stubbed my toe," she answered in a very casual way, which led me to believe she didn't mean it. Something else must have happened. But I knew she didn't want to share it with me. She wanted to keep it hidden.

CHAPTER 9
THE CALL

I kept wondering about the identity of that voice on the phone. I asked my mom so many times, but the only thing she would do was look at my father and whisper, "Maryland." I didn't know what she meant. And she wasn't going to tell me.

I was very confused. We lived in Maryland, but what did Maryland have to do with anything?

I didn't have much time to think about it because I saw a flashing light coming through the window. I knew immediately what it was. I stepped outside, and there it was. The sky was lit up with an eczema ball. The police called me before I could even call them. They explained to me what was happening as I got on my suit.

A man was standing on the top of the Virginia Catwalk Bridge about to take his own life. The eczema ball got me there before it was too late. "Nobody cares about me," he cried.

"I do," I told him. "I am here now because I do. You have a lot more than you realize to live for."

"Everyone who has walked by me has seen that I am about to jump off this bridge but nobody has tried to stop me. Nobody cares."

"That's untrue," I told him. "People have been calling the police nonstop. That is their way of helping you."

"That isn't true," he said. That is when he jumped on-to a ledge that was below him under the bridge. I didn't even have time to think. I threw an eczema ball into the air, I grabbed it with my left hand, and I stretched it as hard as I could. But this time I stretched it out lengthwise, from top to bottom, and I wasn't going to travel in it. I had an idea – hopefully if I didn't step into it, it wouldn't close up into a traveling ball. Instead, I kept it stretched out until it was the length of an eighteen-foot rope. I threw the eczema rope down to the man. He was about ten feet above the wa-ter, but only six feet away from me. I could tell he realized at that point that he wanted to change his mind. He called over and over for help. I screamed to him to grab onto the rope. He grabbed onto it, and I slowly lowered it into the water until the police were able to get him.

The man cried and cried over and over that people re-ally do care about him. He thanked them for saving him, and he thanked me.

As I returned back to my house, I thought about something that never really crossed my mind. I missed my old life . . . my friends, baseball all day, and being normal. I loved being the amazing Eczema Man, but now I have to train and do all of this other stuff all of the time. I wanted my old life back. Just to see my friends. I wanted to go to school with everyone! I was thinking about this when I arrived home. I entered the house and heard the man with the deep voice on the phone again with my mom. This time my dad was standing next to my mom, and he was yelling, "Don't you dare hurt Benny!"

Benny? I had only known one Benny my entire life. My friend Benny who had disappeared. They must have meant someone else. Or maybe they didn't. I always had this weird feeling I would see him again one day.

"What Benny are you talking about?"

My parents looked up toward me, surprised that I was there.

"Do I hear Eczema Man?" I heard the deep voice say into the phone. "Put me on with the kid now!" the man shouted.

My dad put the phone on speaker, handed me the phone, and whispered something to me that sounded like "Maryland."

"Hi Eczema Man. Do you remember me? The man with the Maryland tattoo?" He waited for it to sink in. "That's right. Benny's here with me. He's sleeping right now, but he won't be if you don't meet me Tuesday outside the new IBG (International Big Galactic) Airport in Virginia. Bring

$100,000. If you don't, Benny is done. I will call you at noon on Monday."

He hung up. Just like that.

I could save Benny! Benny was alive! If I was going to use my superhuman powers to do anything, this was the most important thing I could do. I had been practicing reaction times, speed, movement, reflexes, control, and everything I could to be trained for this moment. This is the reason I had to remain Eczema Man.

But why would he call after all of these years? Did he recognize me from the news? Who was he? Why did he call my family and not Benny's? Did he understand my powers?

I asked the same questions to my parents. First my dad said the man probably recognized us from the news and found out information about who we were. So he tracked us down to try to get ransom from us. Maybe he thought we were rich because I was a superhero. Then I noticed something on my dad's arms. Goosebumps. Whenever my dad tried to keep a secret from us, he got the chills and his arms got covered in goose bumps. I could see my dad trying to cover up his arms by crossing them in front of him.

"Nice try dad. What are you covering up?"

I looked at my mom. "Mom, what's going on?"

My mom raised her eyebrows and looked over at my dad. "Honey, it's time we tell him the truth."

At that point, my stomach dropped. What truth? Too many surprises. What was going on? Where was Benny?

"Jimmy, your father and I have been getting messages and calls from the guy who took Benny for the past few days. We think he reached out to us because he recognized you from the news. We don't want to tell the Jaxons until we are sure this is him. We've agreed many times to meet up with him at certain spots. The deal is always the same. We would give him money, and he would give us Benny." Then my dad interrupted, "But he has never shown up."

"This time," my dad said, "he insists he will show up if we bring Eczema Man. We aren't sure why. And we never wanted to involve you in this. We didn't tell the police because we were worried he would hurt Benny."

"Dad, it's okay. I have superhuman powers. I have the police on my side. I can do this. He has no idea what I am capable of doing. Even I am learning new things every day. I can catch him and save Benny. Please . . . just let me do this mom and dad. Please," I begged them.

My parents recommended we call President Jenkins. The very next minute, I called President Jenkins and told him my parents and I needed to speak with him about something very important. He said he would fly in his jet to our house first thing in the morning.

HOLD UP!

So Benny's kidnapper has been in contact with my family, Benny is okay, and my parents didn't tell me. I don't care if they didn't tell me. Benny is actually okay! I have to save him. I will put everything aside in my life to save Benny. I will stop anybody who tries to get in my way. Suddenly after I spoke with my parents, I felt some weird new feelings. I was overcome with sadness, madness, and disgust at the same time. That kidnapping psycho had the nerve to keep in touch with my family and not make any real deals for Benny. He sounded like a real smart aleck. I am going to hurt this guy more than he ever hurt my family and the Jaxons. He will regret this for sure.

When President Jenkins arrived the next morning, the press already was outside of my house. They always seemed to know where the famous people were going to be. Were they also there for me? This was weird.

I got right down to business right after we greeted the President.

"President Jenkins, do you remember the man my mom told you about, the man who took Benny? He has been contacting my parents. He is asking us for a trade. Money for Benny. My parents have been keeping it a secret until they were sure it was real. They also didn't want anyone to get hurt. But this time, the man wants to meet with me, Eczema Man, at IBG Airport on Tuesday. He's going to call me tomorrow with the exact time and location of our meeting spot. I am confident I can do this. I'm prepared, and I'm ready. I must do this."

I continued. "There are three scenarios. I will need police backup for all of them, but I know we can accomplish this task, catch the man, and save Benny. The first scenario is I meet the man, give him the money, the police who are hiding nearby arrest him, and we save Benny. In the second scenario, the man doesn't show up, but we already would have tracked his location when he calls me at noon on Monday. So if he doesn't show up, we can find him, arrest him, and save Benny. In the third scenario, I go alone and fight the man off as Eczema Man, and the police await my call to tell them he's trapped. Of course it is your decision, President Jenkins."

President Jenkins looked at me and didn't answer. I waited. Then a big smile came across his face. "It's amazing to me that a kid can explain a situation so well and actually come up with solutions. It sounds like you have this covered. It's in your hands Jimmy. It's your choice."

"I was thinking we may want to combine Scenario One and Scenario Two," I answered. "We can plan for me to meet him with the money on Tuesday at the planned meeting place. I will take Benny, and the police will be there to arrest the man. If he doesn't show up, it's okay. We already will know his location once we track his phone from the phone call at noon the day before. So the police can arrest him, and we can save Benny."

"Well Jimmy, it may get a bit more complicated. We can track him by his phone, but he may change his location after he calls you or change his phone. So even though he calls from one location and we track it, he may not remain at that location. But I have an idea. We have detectives and investigators who can track him down based on that first phone call. You will need to stay on the phone talking with him long enough for us to track his location. Do you think you can stall him while you talk with him on the phone?

"Sure. I will tell him no plan unless I can speak with Benny. I'll ask him questions. I'll do whatever it takes."

"Once we track down that phone location, we can pinpoint exactly where he is and set up surveillance to watch him. That way even if he doesn't meet you and leaves his location, we will follow him and know exactly where he goes. We will need one of our sketch artists to come by before we go forward with any of these scenarios so you can give them a description of the man. You will need to tell the sketch artist everything you remember even though your memories may have faded from years ago. Tell them whatever you remember about his skin color, eye color, hair color, body type and size, even any tattoos. I know it was a long time ago, so he may look different now. Try to remember as much as you can. Same with Benny. Do you have any photos of Benny?"

"Of course. I keep one next to my bed all of the time. It's the two of us eating ice cream after a baseball game. I will get it now." I ran upstairs and grabbed the photo. I asked if I could get it back because I slept with it on my dresser every night since Benny was taken.

"Absolutely."

I was very worried because it was already Sunday. Tomorrow at noon was the phone call. And on Tuesday, I would have to face the kidnapper. We had a lot to do.

CHAPTER 10
TIME FOR ACTION

HOLD UP!

I know what you're thinking. I must have been petrified. But I was the EXACT OPPOSITE. I was pumped. I had imagined this day for years – the day I would be there to help save Benny. I would do anything for him, and now I had so many special powers and people to help me. This was going to happen, and I would do anything I could to make sure it went flawlessly.

President Jenkins arranged for me to take a break from my training so we could be prepared. The sketch artist came to my house on Sunday afternoon. It was a woman with several tattoos. All of her tattoos were motivational in some way. On her right arm, there was a tattoo that said *Never Give Up* with a picture of Jackie Robinson next to the words. On her left leg, there was a tattoo of Benjamin Franklin that said *Change the World*. I liked her already.

"Hi sweetie. My name is Angie," she said to me in a Southern accent when I entered the living room.

"How are you Miss?"

She smiled. "I'm doing very well honey. Thank you for asking. Now just try your very hardest to remember everything you can about the person. I will ask you some questions, and your only job is to try to visualize the answers in your head. Just explain to me what you see. There's no rush."

I looked at my mom. I think she could tell I was uncomfortable now that I had to focus on the man's face. I had so many nightmares about him for so long. I had tried so hard to forget about him. But he was impossible to forget.

"Now Jimmy, if you are uncomfortable with anything, just say the word banana, and I will ask you something different. Okay hon. I will be asking for as many details as you can give me. Facial hair, tattoos, hair color, eye color, clothing. Anything you can possibly remember about him. Ready to get started?"

I was more than ready.

"Question one: Did you see his face?"

"Yes," I responded, as chills went through by body.

"Question two: Can you describe the shape of his face."

"It was kind of oval, and he had a long chin with a brown goatee on it. I remember thinking he was strange-looking with that goatee."

We went on and on, reviewing every detail I could remember about the man. We spent almost a half hour going over the details of his face before moving on to his body. I described the red tattoo shaped like the state of Maryland on his wrist. I explained how he spoke with a bit of a Southern accent.

"Question thirty two. What was the man wearing on the day of the kidnapping?"

"I remember he was wearing a Becket Pioneers vest. It was navy and said Becket Pioneers in small red letters on the right side of his chest."

And then the questions got much harder. They were about Benny. "Now Jimmy, I know these may be hard for you to answer, but it will help the police very much. So it's very important you remember as much as you can and describe everything in as much detail as you can."

I didn't really want to answer questions about Benny. I could just give them the photo. Wasn't that enough? But I would keep my promise to myself and do everything I could to save him, no matter how difficult it would be.

I just started to talk. "He was the brother I always wanted. He had brown hair and always started conversations by asking, "How was your day?" It was his thing. He would always wear orange."

"That's good," said Angie. "Keep telling me what you can about him."

"He said that instead of having a spirit animal, he had a spirit color, orange. He would always wear stuff that was bright so we could detect him if he got lost. It's almost as if he predicted he would be taken."

I continued, "I guess what he wore the day he was taken doesn't matter now; it wouldn't fit him anymore. He had lots and lots of freckles. He was skinny, though he had big feet. His father Martin said it meant he would be tall like his grandfather. His shoes may have been a size four when he was only five years old."

A man walked over to us and handed Angie a photo. I was startled when he handed it to her because I hadn't even seen or heard him coming. I was thinking so deeply about Benny. It was the photo of the two of us together eating ice cream.

"Is this Benny standing in this photo with you? Is this what Benny looked like?" Angie asked me.

"That's him. We took that about two weeks before our trip. We were eating ice cream and talking all about the games we would go to and the players we would see."

"Well Jimmy, if this is how you remember Benny, I can use this photo to help me with the sketch. Would that be easier for you?"

"Probably." I felt relieved.

When Angie was done, I couldn't believe the resemblance. She drew the man almost exactly the way I remembered him. But something was different. I kept looking at the sketch of the man to figure out what it was that looked different. She put him in the Becket Pioneers vest, and he had all of the features I described. But something was still different. I thought about it and told her the man's hair in the sketch had some white in it. The real man's hair actually was brown. I also told her this man looked really tired in the sketch, something about his eyes.

"That's because I am drawing what he would look like now, a few years older. This is what the man who took Benny would probably look like after all of these years and time." I understood and thanked her. I left in a hurry. I wanted to think this all out and be really prepared. I was heading with my parents to the police station when I created a nickname for the man who stole Benny. Professor Kidnap.

When we got to the station, police officers were coming up to me and thanking me for helping the city. I kept thanking them for their service. Then I sat down with the Chief of Police and five police officers, and we made a plan. I would find out the details over the phone on Monday at noon. The police would be listening in on the call. I would try to stall Professor Kidnap during our conversation so the police could try to track his location. I was going to insist I speak with Benny or threaten to call off the deal. I was going to ask him what they would be wearing. I was going to ask him what type of bills he wanted. I was going to be sure we spoke long enough so the police would have enough time to track his location from his phone.

On Tuesday, I would meet with Professor Kidnap at our planned location. As soon as he handed over Benny, I would act like I was handing him a briefcase with the money in it. Instead, I would shoot Professor Kidnap with eczema in the legs many times to freeze him in his tracks. I would say a certain code word into a secret microphone that was disguised to look like a button on my suit. At that point, the police would come and arrest Professor Kidnap, and I would take Benny and the briefcase to a safe place.

If Professor Kidnap didn't show up, we would have traced the call the day before and found out his location. The police would have been watching him starting Monday to be sure they knew where he was at all times. That way, if he stood me up on Tuesday or changed his location, the police would know where he was and go, arrest him, and rescue Benny.

We decided to stick with Scenario One first. We wanted Benny with Professor Kidnap out in the open so I could know Benny was safe before handing over the briefcase. Also, if anything went wrong, it would be easier for the police to move in and save Benny if it all happened out in the open. Either way, Benny would be found and saved, and Professor Kidnap would be in jail.

HOLD UP!

Yes, I know that I'm interrupting the story again. And I know you want to find out what happens next. But you have got to admit that it's a win, win plan. It can't fail, right?

By the way, I wasn't sure what to say for the code word. I was given permission to ask Anthony for advice. I called him and briefly explained my situation. I think he was in shock about the whole thing. Then I asked, "Any recommendations for what the code word should be?"

I expected him to make it something dumb or to make a silly joke out of it. But he didn't. "What are your five favorite things?" he asked.

I paused a minute and thought about my five favorite things:

1. Eczema
2. Baseball
3. Family
4. Friends
5. Superhumans

"That's it!" Anthony exclaimed. "That's your code word. Take the first letter of each of your five favorite things and make a word out of them. B.E.F.F.S."

Anthony's idea made perfect sense! My word would be Beffs!

By the way, the phone call went as planned. Professor Kidnap called my parents' phone at noon on Monday. He told me to meet him at the yellow column in the parking lot next to the airplane hangar near the international flight area at 10am on Tuesday. I told him I had to speak with Benny before he hung up or no deal. I almost cried when he put Benny on the phone. Benny sounded exactly the same. He was only allowed to say hi. But hearing him say my name was my motivation to be sure Professor Kidnap would be put away forever.

I then told Professor Kidnap I wanted to be sure he was satisfied (don't you like my reverse psychology?). I asked him what types of bills he wanted and if putting them in a briefcase was okay. He talked in detail about the way he wanted the money. He was very specific about the exact amounts of hundreds, twenties and tens he wanted. (This guy really was crazy!)

By that point, the Chief of Police who was in my house standing next to me during the call gave me a thumbs up. They had traced Professor Kidnap's location. Now he could be under surveillance. It was time!

Now back to the story . . .

CHAPTER 11

TWO DAYS LATER: THE FIGHT

As I got to the IBG Airport, I could smell evil in the air. Taste evil. And even hear evil. "I've been waiting to kill you, the town's precious superhero. The fabulous Eczema Man."

The voice was high and mocking. I looked around, but nobody else seemed to hear it. I spoke into the button microphone to the police. "Do you guys hear his voice?"

"No, can't hear anything Jimmy."

I realized it was like the screaming in the supermarket. My mom couldn't hear it, but I could.

"You and I both know that the town hero is just a worthless little boy who can't stop anyone without his puny eczema hands."

He was trying to rile me up for his own pleasure. But I knew something he didn't. When you mess with me, you mess with more than Jimmy. You mess with Eczema Man.

I was wearing my suit, and I was holding the briefcase. I had my button set up on my suit. I was prepared mentally. This was it. And I could tell by the sound of his voice – this time he showed up.

I approached the yellow column, and there was Professor Kidnap with Benny. Professor Kidnap was wearing that same dumb vest, and Angie was right. He looked older. But I mostly focused on Benny. Professor Kidnap was holding him by the arm. Benny looked so scared as I walked up to them. But as soon as Benny saw me, his eyes widened, and he made a little smile. I looked at him and smiled back, trying to let him know everything would be okay.

"I have the briefcase right here. But hand over Benny to me first."

"Fine."

Professor Kidnap started to walk toward me while holding tightly onto Benny's arm. He was playing right into my plan. He started to hand over Benny, and I shot as quickly as I could three eczema blasts at Professor Kidnap's legs.

He dodged the first one but got hit in the legs with the second and third. I grabbed Benny. I got him!

But suddenly, Professor Kidnap reached into his vest pocket and pulled out a long thin rod with steam coming out of the end of it. It looked like some type of gun. He aimed it at me for about a second. My heart stopped.

I was waiting for the police to react. Within a second, however, Professor Kidnap turned the rod downward, aimed it at his own legs, and shot at both of his legs. He shot himself twice! What!

"You see Eczema Man. You are still just a little boy with puny eczema hands. I already knew you were going to have police backup. I knew you would try to trap me in your eczema. But this heat gun reaches the highest temperatures you can imagine. One thousand two hundred fifty six degrees Fahrenheit to be exact. Up until now, nobody could penetrate your eczema traps. UNTIL NOW I SAID!" He laughed in such an evil way that my ears stung.

"This heat not only will dissolve your eczema trap. It will remove any eczema from my body so there is no impact on my cells. And I won't even get burned from the heat thanks to you. Your eczema forms a shield so strong that the heat melts only the eczema and not my body. Thanks Jimmy!"

I wasn't sure if the police were listening and whether they were coming. It seemed like forever, and this definitely was not part of our plan.

"You see, I've studied your every move. I've read every article about you, researched every detail about eczema, and understand every one of your weaknesses. I've even dressed up as a reporter and stood outside your house as you and President Jenkins plotted against me. So you see, Little Jimmy, while you were worried about me, I wasn't worried about you."

"BEFFS!!!" I shouted into the button. Police cars swarmed around us within seconds as I ran toward them with Benny as quickly as I could. I hugged Benny so hard and told him how much I missed him. We both cried.

The plan had been for me to grab Benny and bring him to safety while the police arrested Professor Kidnap. But this twist made it a bit more complicated. Would the police be able to catch Professor Kidnap now that he melted the eczema, grabbed the briefcase, and ran toward his car to escape? As he was about to jump into his car, the loudest, most annoying, high-pitched sound started to ring in my ears. It was like those screeching fireworks that shoot straight up into the sky before they explode into a colorful fountain of color. No, it was more like a crying so loud that it hurt my head. My ears were killing, and my forehead started to pound. Eeeeeeeeeeeek. It wouldn't stop.

"You don't like loud sounds do you, Jimmy? Well neither did I, but I had no choice during that plane ride to California, did I Jimmy?"

I could barely understand what he was saying.

"You see little eczema boy, I told you I studied everything about you leading up to this day. You may have Benny, but I have the money, and I know your weaknesses. So I have you. I am a mastermind. You can't defeat me. You will never win. I know you can't tolerate high pitched sounds." And with that, Professor Kidnap was gone.

But we had Benny!

CHAPTER 12

AGONY OF DEFEAT

*T*he next day, Benny's family and mine had dinner at my house. Benny and I went into the backyard to catch up. It had been so long. We almost didn't know where to start. We laughed about old baseball stories. I told him all about school and our old friends. Just like my friends didn't ask me questions when I was training, I didn't ask Benny any questions about Professor Kidnap. The police psychologist told me that Benny would open up when he was ready.

Out of the blue, Benny announced to me, "Last night I ate three chicken tenders and a milkshake." I looked at him funny. He probably realized how odd it was that he would blurt out to me what he ate for dinner. We both started to crack up. We cracked up so hard that we couldn't stop. But deep down, I was sad. I knew what he meant. It had been so long since he ate the way my friends and I did.

Then I had an idea! Benny was with Professor Kidnap for years. He probably knew more than anyone about Professor Kidnap. Benny could be a hero too. He could help provide the government with information to take down the evilest man I knew. I didn't want to share my idea with Benny in case the psychologist thought it was too much for him to handle. I pulled out my phone. "Sophie, can you remind me tomorrow morning at 8am to call President Jenkins?"

"Okay. I'll remind you."

Benny looked at me like I was crazy. He stared at the phone in absolute disbelief. Did the phone just talk to you? What in the world . . . ?"

Wow. I hadn't realized how long it had been. The next few hours flew by. I told Benny about Sophie and all of the other inventions that would fascinate him. At least it got his mind off of Professor Kidnap.

CHAPTER 13

REUNITING

HOLD UP!

By the way, before we go on, I want to tell you about a little secret we have planned for Benny. You can't tell anyone. We're having a surprise party for him. All of his friends and relatives are going to be going to his house for a surprise dinner. Now go and enjoy the story. I won't spoil the rest for you.

Benny got really quiet at one point while we were sitting together in my living room. He looked at me seriously and said something kind of weird. "I have a question to ask you, but you don't have to answer it if you don't want to. I mean, you can tell me, and I won't say anything. Or you don't have to tell me at all. Or you can tell me part of it and not all of it."

He was confusing me. "Ask me whatever you want."

"The other day some weird stuff came out of your hands. It looked like you were going to throw a baseball, and all of a sudden, it shot out of your hands. What was it cuz it stuck "him" to the ground?"

"Benny, I can tell you, but if I do, I may need your help to catch him. I call "him" Professor Kidnap by the way." I went into detail about what happened during the baseball game. I explained how I saved the lady by the field. I explained the grocery store and the bridge. I shared all of the details I was allowed to share. I just didn't tell the secrets about my training and private meetings with important people.

"So you are the one who saved that man from jumping off the bridge? No way! Do you have some type of super-powers! Can you fly? Can you become invisible? Can you eat as many sweets as you want and not get sick? Are you indestructible?"

I cracked up. But I probably would have asked the same questions. "Benny, I'm not indestructible. You can ask me whatever you want, as long as you promise not to tell anyone."

"I promise. I promise." Before I could even respond, he started to ask even more questions. "Is Randy okay? (By the way, Randy was the catcher who got covered in eczema the very first time I discovered my powers. Benny, Randy, and I grew up playing little league together). Do you meet important people? Are you ever scared?"

"Randy is okay. The BIA did some tests on him, and he is fine. I am not usually scared, though I was scared the other day when Professor Kidnap pulled out that gun. As for important people, I know this may sound crazy, but I am friends with President Jenkins and Adam Hamel."

"The President of the United States! Wow! But who is Adam Hamel?"

That's when it really hit me that Benny's life must have been so isolated and lonely. He lost most of his childhood. I told him Hamel's the greatest pitcher I've ever seen.

"Want me to show you some of his pitches?"

"How? We aren't at a game?"

I pulled out my cell phone and showed him videos of some of Hamel's highlights. He was amazed! "Let's talk about this later," I told Benny. "Let's go play some catch outside."

Benny clearly wanted to play catch. He ran out of my room and down the stairs, grabbed his baseball gear, put on his shoes, and waited in the kitchen for me to catch up. Once we got outside, we started to throw the ball to each other. But none of Benny's throws were even close to me. It was almost as if he forgot how to throw a baseball. I moved in about twenty feet until we were super close. Then I threw as slowly as I could. As he got the hang of it, I backed up more and more and threw harder and harder. It all came back to him. Soon he was throwing accurately to me at almost 45 mph. "You are ready to go back on the field my friend!"

Benny gave me the biggest smile I had seen since he got home. I asked him if he wanted to sleep over, the way he used to, but he said he needed to help his parents with something at home. I understood. I knew he didn't have to help them with anything because they told me it would be okay for me to ask him to spend the night. I guessed he just wasn't ready yet.

Then all of a sudden, he started to open up to me. "In the mornings with him, I mean Professor Kidnap, I would put on my clothes and cook breakfast. I slept on a couch with a blanket, but it wasn't even half my size. Then I had to go to the backyard to feed all four of his bulldogs. He would always go outside and rough them up before I fed them. I'm not sure why, but most of the time when I fed them, they would bite my hand. It hurt a lot." Benny showed me his left had. It was covered with bruises. Then he started to cry.

"It's okay Benny. We don't have to talk about it."

"Then I would clean the house. Most days he would lock the door and hide the key. If I tried to leave, an alarm would sound. He never hit me or hurt me. But one time, when he left the house, I saw the alarm wasn't on. I took the key and ran as far away as I could. I saw a police car and waved and waved at it screaming for help. It was about 8:30 at night. When the police car turned around, I was so happy. I couldn't believe it. Maybe the policeman would recognize me from flyers or the news. I was sure my family was looking for me. I knew they would never give up."

"Suddenly, the man, I mean Professor Kidnap, pulled up in his pick up truck. 'I'm so sorry Officer Sir,' Professor Kidnap said in his nicest voice. He called me Sammy. He turned to me and said, 'Sammy, I can't believe you got lost this late at night. I thought you knew how to get home from your cousin's house. You must have had your mind on your birthday party.'"

Benny continued, "I had no idea what he was talking about. And who was Sammy? I was confused so I didn't say anything to the Officer. Then Professor Kidnap told me to get into the truck, politely thanked the police officer, and drove off."

"I cried the whole way home. Professor Kidnap didn't say a word. Instead, he made my life even worse. He would make me embarrass myself in front of his friends. I would have to dance, sing or tell them jokes. I was humiliated. He never forgot to turn on the door alarm after that."

I felt so bad for Benny. I knew no matter how hard I tried, I couldn't understand his pain. He was trapped for years, with no love or comfort. I needed to help him get his mind off of all of this and make him smile again. I knew something was about to happen that would make him really happy. Remember the surprise?

My mom and Benny's mom, Francine, were busy setting up next door at the Jaxons for the big surprise. I tried my hardest to keep Benny away from that area. All of Benny's old friends were arriving at 5:00. There was an ice cream bar set up next to the pizza. There was a foosball table and air hockey. We even had a piñata filled with all of Benny's favorite candies. Wimple Gobbers, Super Loppers, and Mini Timmy's. All of Benny's family friends and relatives were going to be at the party. My job was to keep Benny busy so he couldn't figure it out.

Finally at 5:20, I stuck to the plan. I asked Benny if we could go next door and see Cocoa, his labrador retriever. Cocoa was so excited when Benny first returned home. It seemed like Cocoa totally remembered Benny. It was amazing. Cocoa smelled him, jumped up on him, licked him, and didn't leave Benny's side.

Everyone was asked to park around the corner for the surprise party so Benny wouldn't become suspicious if our block was loaded with parked cars near his house. Benny turned the doorknob to his front door, expecting Cocoa to run up to us. Instead, he heard the loudest chorus ever of SURPRISE! Benny was so thrilled. He was grinning from ear to ear. "Who wants cake?" his mom shouted just as thrilled. "BENNY'S HOME!"

Everyone ran into the dining room where a huge vanilla cake with blue frosting spelled out WELCOME HOME BENNY! After cake, Benny smacked the piñata harder than most people on the baseball team could. I think it was a combination of happiness and a release of pain and sadness. He smacked, and smacked, and smacked. He smacked long after the piñata cracked open. He smacked even when it was on the floor, detached from its string. I could tell he really needed that. Candy poured all over the floor, and everyone scrambled for it. Benny was able to have fun. Everyone was hugging him, telling him how they missed him, and welcoming him home.

HOLD UP!

I had a special surprise of my own planned. I ran upstairs and put on my suit. The plan was for me to hide behind the stairs. My dad would announce a special guest was here to welcome Benny home, and I would pop out from under the staircase. After that, I would ask Benny to come in front of everyone and help me with a trick. I would hand him a baseball and he would toss it up. While the baseball was in the air, I would then pitch eczema at the ball with all of my might. But the best part of the trick that I practiced over and over was the way I would throw the eczema ball. I would throw a special curved eczema ball that not only was fast and powerful, but when it intercepted Benny's ball, it would boomerang both right back to me. And then I would hand both balls to Benny. (*I actually tested this out with my Dad a couple of times to be sure it would work*).

It's good I practiced it ahead of time with my dad. Unfortunately, not everything always goes as planned. Let's just say whoever says practice makes perfect was not lying. I definitely am glad I practiced! At first, my dad would throw a baseball, and I would be so off that my curveball would end up covering a tree or the car in eczema. One time, I even destroyed my mom's new vase. But after about twenty-five tries, I got much better at it. I started to play around with trick shots. My dad would toss up a baseball, and I would intercept it in the air with an eczema ball that transformed into a lasso of eczema. I would pull my dad's ball back to me in the lasso of eczema.

Now was the real thing. My dad announced that a special guest had arrived. I popped out from under the staircase ready to call up Benny to the front of the room. But suddenly, I heard a buzzing. It was loud and really irritated my ears. It sounded frighteningly familiar. Then it suddenly disappeared, and I heard a ticking. It started out quiet, but the ticking got louder and louder and louder. It sounded like a clock was right up to my ear. Soon I couldn't focus on my own thoughts because the ticking was so painful.

Suddenly the buzzing started again. This time I had a bad feeling – I recognized that buzzing. It sounded evil. I had heard that sound only one time before. I knew it wasn't good. I realized what the ticking had to be. "EVERYONE GET DOWN!" I yelled at the top of my lungs.

"BOOM!" The ground rumbled. The whole entire house shook. Vases and pictures fell off of the shelves and walls. The ceiling started to crumble. People were holding their ears and hiding under tables. A bomb had detonated under the house.

"Did you really think you could get away from me before I finished you off?" I recognized the voice, but I couldn't get up. It was Professor Kidnap. My ears were ringing, and my head was throbbing. "I screwed up last time. Giving you back your perfect little friend. But now you will pay Jimmy Mancini." I heard my name just as he walked toward me.

"How do you even know who I am?" I asked him.

"You are all that little brat Benny talked about night and day for weeks until I forbid it. As if he wasn't noisy enough during that horrific flight to California. I had to listen to your name day and night. You ruined my peace again and again and again." He paused. "When I finally had some peace and quiet, your face suddenly showed up on every news channel . . . Jimmy Mancini, the big hero. I knew immediately it was you before I even heard your name. And I promised myself I would get my revenge!"

"Now where was I at?" Professor Kidnap continued. "Oh, yes. Finishing you off."

Right then and there, he pulled out a gun and pointed it at me. Right before he could shoot, I jumped behind the nearest table. I heard a bang, but I didn't feel anything. Was I hit? I wondered if that's what it is supposed to feel like when you get hit by a gun. Does the pain come later?

"Warm up shot," said Professor Kidnap. Now that people knew my name, they started to chant, "Jimmy, Jimmy, Jimmy." It got louder and louder, but it didn't stop Professor Kidnap. He was about to fire another shot. This time I jumped to the side of where he aimed, hoping he would miss again, when Benny approached Professor Kidnap from behind and did something I never thought would happen. He snuck up behind Professor Kidnap, grabbed him by the back of the shirt, kicked the gun out of Professor Kidnap's hand, bent down and picked it up, and let out all of his emotions. He pointed the gun at Professor Kidnap. "You kept me against my will. You separated me from my friends and family. I suffered every day. You robbed me of my childhood. I didn't have friends, I didn't get to do the things other kids did, and I missed my life."

"Please help me," begged Professor Kidnap. "Please, Eczema Man. If you are a hero, you will save me. Benny is going to kill me. You've got to save me."

"That's the difference between you and me," said Benny. I know right from wrong. You taught me what's wrong, and my parents taught me what's right."

Benny and I looked at each other, and it was clear. Nothing had changed. We understood one another without even having to speak. We both nodded, and Benny quickly stepped out of the way.

I pitched an eczema ball as hard as I could with all of my might. The eczema covered Professor Kidnap. I called the police, and Professor Kidnap remained frozen until the police arrived. I heard that by the time he became unfrozen, he was in a jail cell.

CHAPTER 14

EVERYTHING THAT STARTS MUST COME TO AN END

During the past few months, I have reached many goals and grown as a person . . . A LOT! I have superpowers I never could have imagined. I have fought and taken down criminals. I have saved lives. I have won baseball games – with my right AND my left hand. And most of all, I found Benny.

Benny is more than a freckled, brown-haired baseball player. He is resilient and brave. He is strong and committed. He is funny and happy. He is ethical and honest. And I love hearing him ask, "How was your day?" every morning when we walk to school.

Everyday I am thankful for the one thing I always dreaded. I used to look down at my hands and hate the itchy feeling and peeling of my eczema. I wondered why I had to deal with this miserable discomfort. I hated being different and people always asking me what was wrong with me.

So you ask . . . do I feel that way anymore? NO WAY! Eczema is probably the best thing that ever happened to me, except for finding Benny. After Benny's surprise party, I realized he and I really understand each other. And he actually is pretty good at this Eczema Man stuff. Every superhero needs a sidekick, right?

CPSIA information can be obtained
at www.ICGtesting.com
Printed in the USA
LVHW091805150621
690286LV00007B/1257